To Willa +
Briney
Love Grammy

THE
HUMBLE STONE

THE HUMBLE STONE

David Paulus

Illustrated by Linda Wuest

• Barnsley Ink •
RALEIGH, NORTH CAROLINA

• BARNSLEY INK •
RALEIGH, NORTH CAROLINA

For my grandaughter Callie Grace,
our little heart warrior.
– David

To my grandson Luke, you are
strong and courageous!
– Linda

As the sun rose each morning while eagles soared past his towering cliffs, Petros looked down at the hills, valleys, and sparkling streams and proudly announced, "I am the highest peak as far as the eye can see. I am majestic to behold!"

He never tired of boasting how magnificent he was.

"Look up at my peak and you will see, nothing around compares with me!"

A chorus from the surrounding hills would always answer,

"You boast of your greatness to us all,
but when your pride peaks,
you soon will fall!"

Petros ignored the wisdom from the hills. Instead, he continued his boasting.

"Look up at my peak and you will see,
nothing around compares with me!"

But secretly Petros was unhappy and lonely.

One sunny afternoon, Petros heard a loud **RUMBLE**, then felt a small **CRUMBLE**.

He was startled when he began to shake and the ground began to **QUAKE** as the **RUMBLE** grew louder and **louder**.

CRAACCKKK!!!

"AAAAHHH!"

screamed Petros as he toppled over and found himself crashing down the mountainside.

Picking up speed, he was **SMASHING** into rocks and boulders, pieces chipping and flying, as he **PLUMMETED**

toward the valley below!

"Ooh, ow! Ouch! Ouch!"

he cried as he felt himself getting **smaller** and **smaller** and smaller until he finally landed.

KERPLLLUNK!

"What just happened? Where am I?" Petros wondered.

He looked around. He had tumbled into the middle of a stream in a valley. Water was dancing and splashing over him. He was no longer a majestic mountain peak high in the air. Now the bottom of this stream was his new home!

Days, then years passed as Petros rested in the stream. The flowing water slowly wore away his jagged edges. Little by little he felt himself changing. One day Petros noticed he had become a small, smooth stone. Petros sighed.

"Everything is higher than me! I will never be majestic again! I will never do anything great!"

As time continued to pass, Petros thought, "Perhaps the hills, valleys, and streams have their own majesty too." Petros was learning to be humble!

He realized his prideful boasting had not made him happy when he was a magnificent mountain peak. He found that being humble allowed him to enjoy the other stones around him. As they rested together beneath the cool, gurgling waters, Petros let his dreams of being mighty drift away. He was happy and content.

Then one day without warning,

SPLASH!

Petros saw the hand of a young boy plunge into the water. He felt himself being snatched from the stream.

In a blink, he was dropped into a leather pouch with four other smooth stones.

It was dark inside the pouch. Petros did not know what was happening! Huddling together in the darkness, he and the other stones heard a booming, arrogant voice boasting of his strength and defying the armies of Israel.

Petros thought, "I **was once boastful. I must have sounded just like him!**" He remembered the chorus from the hills.

"**You boast of your greatness to us all, but when your pride peaks, you soon will . . .**"

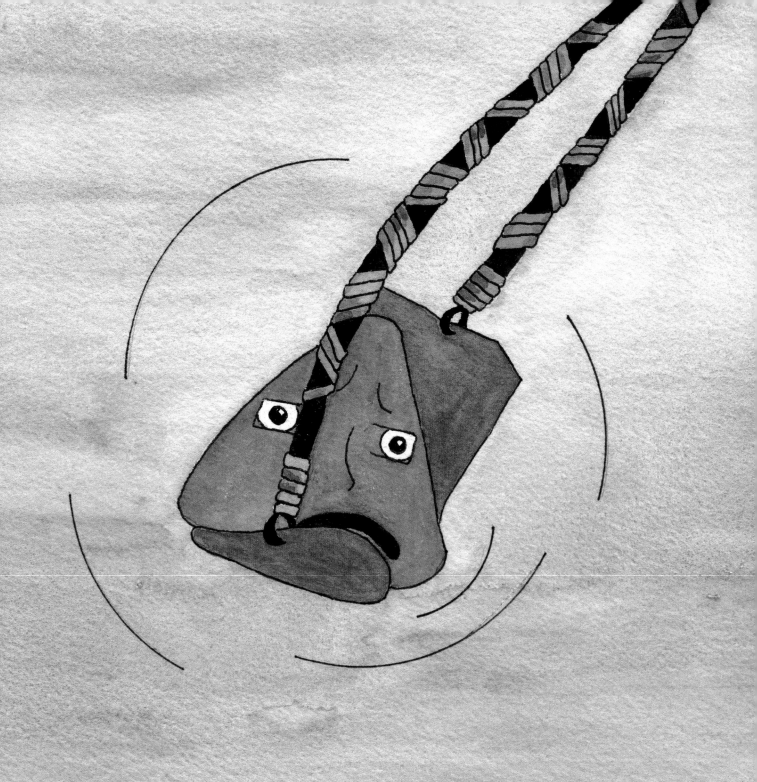

Before Petros finished his thought, the young boy's hand plucked him from the pouch and placed him in a sling.

Round and round and round Petros went. Faster and faster and faster he circled until the sling hurled him toward its target.

"Whooooaa!"

screamed Petros as he streaked through the air.

THUNK!

Petros slammed into the forehead
of the giant shouting his boasts.

The giant crashed to the ground. Frightened by his fall, the giant's army fled to the hills!

There was loud cheering from the armies of Israel as the young boy picked up Petros and marveled.

"Oh, humble little stone, the Living God of Israel helped us defeat the evil giant Goliath and his army who stood against us. Today God has used you for a great and mighty purpose!"

Then the young boy lifted Petros high into the air for the celebrating armies of Israel to see. Petros, once a lofty mountain peak, looked down at the victorious crowd and was filled with joy at the happy faces all around him.

A humble little stone had done what a mountain could not—

a mighty act!

ABOUT THE AUTHOR

When I was a young child, my mother introduced me to the excitement and wonder of children's literature, which I found fascinating. For most of my adult life I contemplated writing for children. Having mentally structured the bones of a tale to introduce young children to virtuous living, I always found a reason not to write it. One evening this past year my wife and I were dinner guests at our neighbors' home. In conversation, my desire to write a children's book surfaced. While explaining the overarching theme and outline of the story, eyes lit up around the table and encouraging voices agreed that the story should be written. Out of excuses, the following morning my thumbs were tapping on my iPhone and within a couple hours, the first draft of *The Humble Stone* was completed.

This is the first book in a series of stories that will focus on showing children how to grow in virtue. It is my sincere hope that a warm dialogue will develop between parents and children while reading this entertaining account of one journey toward humility.

ABOUT THE ILLUSTRATOR

Linda Wuest is an artist who followed her childhood dream of studying art at The University of Texas. She ultimately, however, became a nurse, always maintaining

her passion for her art. She continued to paint and found ways to share her art with her patients at the cancer center by creating murals at Christmastime and other projects for their ACS Relay for Life team. She now paints full-time in acrylic, alcohol ink, and water color. She is a member of several online art communities, and her water color won the Craftsy Winter Spotlight Challenge in 2017. Her passion is to create art that reflects Scripture and Worship Music, sharing God's message of hope and joy with the world. When David Paulus read his story *The Humble Stone* to her, she was so moved by the message that she knew she wanted to create the art for this wonderful story!

ACKNOWLEDGMENTS

The sincerest form of gratitude cannot adequately express my indebtedness to my wife, Maria, for encouraging me to write this story. During the past 30 years, she has lovingly prodded me to write while confidently cheering me on. She remains my most ardent and steadfast advocate.

Tremendous support has also come from the following individuals who helped to adjust key elements of the story and made numerous proofing suggestions. Profound appreciation goes to my daughter, Rachel, daughter-in-law, Katelyn, and friends Kay Reviere and Karen Fletcher for their candid nudging. They all assisted in chiseling away at the stone to reveal the story beneath.

After initially hearing the story, Linda Wuest's goosebumps were the catalyst for her request to illustrate *The Humble Stone*. I'm most thankful she desired the role as her delightful art has helped to bring the story to life!

I'm also grateful to Lee Heinrich, my publisher, editor, and exceedingly patient instructor in the finer points of writing for children. She is the glue that has held this project together.

Finally, I am pleased to acknowledge Dr. Gloria Malone, retired English professor from Mount Union College (today, the University of Mount Union), for her inspiration and unceasing demand for excellence. It is she who helped deepen my love for children's literature! — *DP*

I am incredibly thankful for the overwhelming support of my amazing husband, Skip, to pursue my life-long dream of being an artist full time! His encouragement for me to follow my artistic passion has been the fuel that has propelled me along this journey. Over the past year of developing the art-work for this story, he has always been there to cheer me on. Many thanks also to David Paulus for allowing me the opportunity to create the visual backdrop for his delightful and compelling story. I would also like to acknowledge all of my family, and especially Ellie, Claire, Luke, and Blake, my grandchildren, for being my inspiration for making art with the message of the hope and joy we have in the Lord! — *LW*

Made in the USA
Monee, IL
16 August 2020